SPRING IS

PICTURES BY JANINA DOMANSKA

GREENWILLOW BOOKS

A DIVISION OF WILLIAM MORROW & COMPANY, INC. / NEW YORK

Printed in the United States of America.   1 2 3 4 5 80 79 78 77 76
LIBRARY OF CONGRESS CATALOGING IN PUBLICATION DATA
Domanska, Janina.   Spring is.
Summary: A small dog explores the fields in the four seasons.   [1.   Seasons—Fiction]
I.   Title.   PZ7.D710Sp   [E]   75-25953   ISBN O-688-80026-2   ISBN O-688-84026-4 lib. bdg.

To Witold
with love

Spring is showery,

flowery,

bowery.

Summer is

hoppy,

poppy,

floppy.

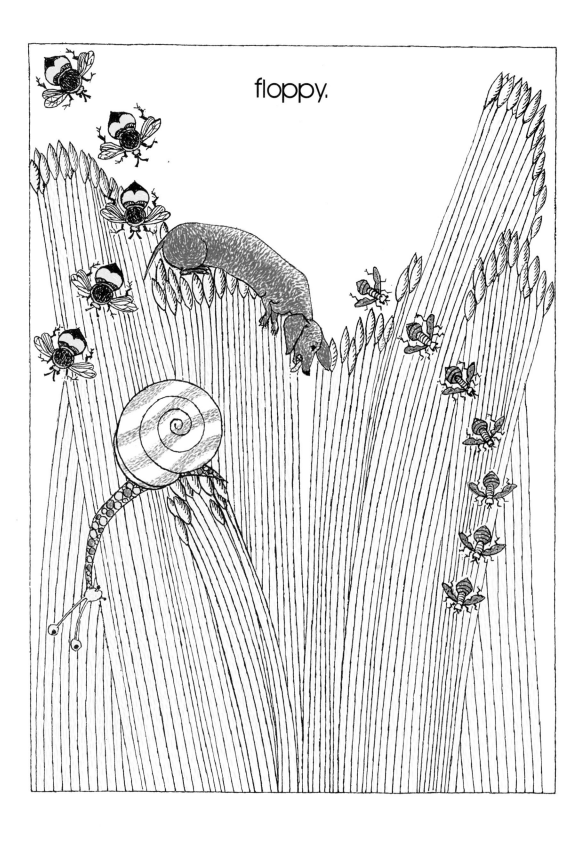

Autumn is

wheezy,

sneezy,

freezy.

Winter is

slippy,

drippy,

nippy.

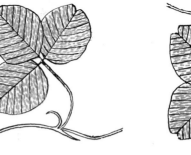

E
Dom   Domanska, Janina
            Spring is

	DATE DUE		
SEP 28 '88			
SEP 26 '89			
MAR 27 '90			
MAR 30 '90			
MAR 30 '90			
APR 10 '92			
JAN 17 '95			
APR 7 '96